LUCY
TAKES A
HOLIDAY

For information contact:
MONDO Publishing
One Plaza Road, Greenvale, NY 11548
Visit our web site at http://www.mondopub.com

Printed in Hong Kong
98 99 00 01 02 03 04   9 8 7 6 5 4 3 2 1

Designed by Mina Greenstein
Production by The Kids at Our House

Library of Congress Cataloging-in-Publication Data
Murdocca, Salvatore.
    Lucy takes a holiday / Salvatore Murdocca.
        p.   cm.
    Summary: Lucy the dog gets tired of her family and decides to take a well-deserved vacation trip to Dogwood Island.
        ISBN 1-57255-560-2 (hardcover : alk. paper). — ISBN 1-57255-561-0 (pbk. : alk. paper)
        [1. Dogs—Fiction.   2. Vacations—Fiction.]   I. Title.
PZ7.M94Lu   1998
[Fic]—DC21   97-10789
                                                    CIP
                                                    AC

LUCY
TAKES A
HOLIDAY

SALVATORE MURDOCCA

MONDO

Lucy was having the worst day ever.
It was so hot, all she wanted was to
be left alone in a nice shady spot.
But everything was going wrong.
Barbara made Lucy run and fetch
a tennis ball about a hundred times.
Then Anthony found Lucy's Frisbee,
and she spent the next hour
running and leaping.

Dog tired, Lucy lay down to rest. Just then the little boy from up the street gave her tail a playful tug.

Well, before she could stop herself, Lucy gave the boy a piece of her mind.

"Grrrr-ruff!" she barked indignantly, and suddenly the boy was running home.

A few minutes later the boy returned
with his father.

"Your dog's got a mean temper," the
boy's father said to Mother.

"Bad dog!" Mother scolded Lucy.

Lucy was so embarrassed! She felt like
howling, but she lowered her head
instead and tried to show she was sorry.

That night Lucy could not sleep. So just
before sunrise, she packed a suitcase. Then
she walked to the bus stop.

About five minutes later a huge bus
appeared out of nowhere.
"Is this the bus to Dog Town?" Lucy asked.

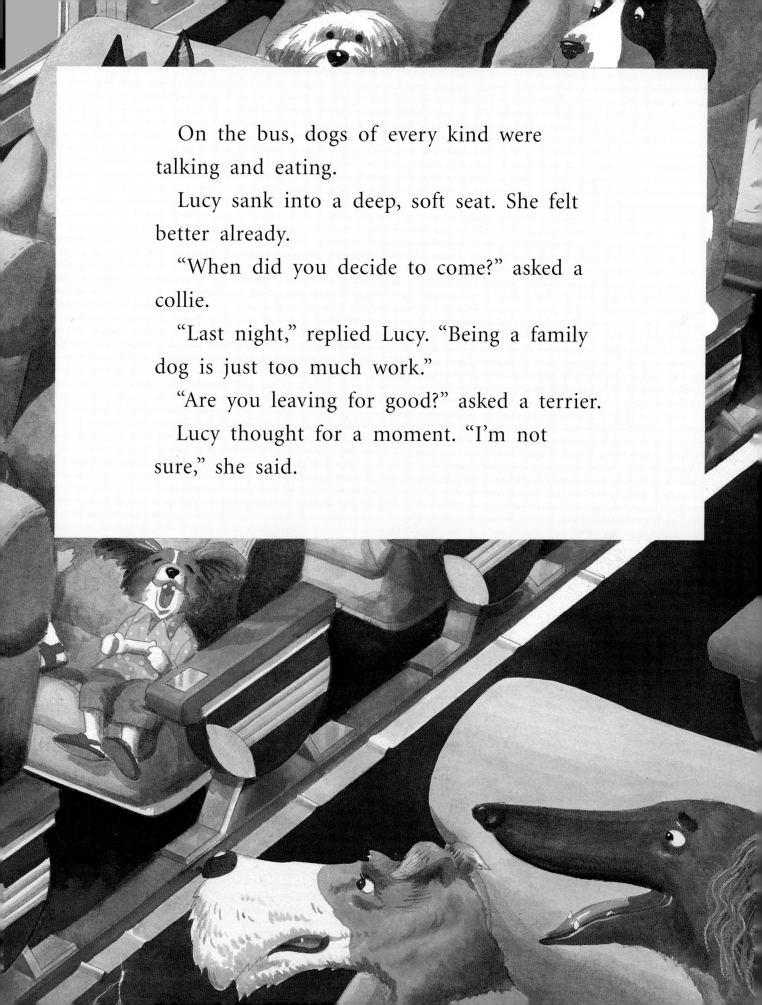

On the bus, dogs of every kind were talking and eating.

Lucy sank into a deep, soft seat. She felt better already.

"When did you decide to come?" asked a collie.

"Last night," replied Lucy. "Being a family dog is just too much work."

"Are you leaving for good?" asked a terrier.

Lucy thought for a moment. "I'm not sure," she said.

It was beginning to grow light when the bus pulled into Dog Town and parked by a ferry boat. Lucy got off and followed the cheerful pack onto the ferry.

As the ferry pulled away from the dock Lucy ran straight to the bow. She wanted to feel the salty wind on her nose.

BARKING MERMAID

Two hours later green mountains appeared on the horizon. It wasn't long before Lucy could see the coast of Dogwood Island.

An English setter nudged Lucy.

"This is the only place to come when you're tired of being a family dog," said the setter.

Lucy checked into a hotel by the beach.

"Are you looking for a permanent dog house?" asked the clerk.

"I'm not sure," replied Lucy.

Lucy took a room overlooking the ocean.
Soon the sea air made her sleepy.

After a short nap Lucy went to town. She spotted a beautiful pair of earrings.

"These would look lovely on your long ears," said the shopkeeper. "Please help yourself."

It was then that Lucy realized everything on Dogwood Island was free.

Lucy went into the beauty parlor.

"You have marvelous hair," said the hairdresser.

The next three days were some of the
happiest of Lucy's life.

On the first day she went scuba diving.

On the second day she went sailing.

On the third day she went mountain biking.

And she went dancing every night.

On the third evening Lucy and her
friends went to Coyote Park. They rode all
the rides, had their photographs taken, and
Lucy even won a singing contest.

Later, while walking on the beach,
Lucy and her friends decided to play
Frisbee.

After making a wonderful catch Lucy
stopped short.

"Is anything wrong?" asked the collie.

"It's time to go home," replied Lucy.
"I miss my family and my Frisbee."

The next afternoon, all the dogs on the island came to see Lucy off. The sea breeze dried the happy tears in her eyes.

Almost everybody slept on the bus ride home.

Lucy sniffed the air as the bus
approached her neighborhood. "Home,"
she said softly to herself.

After putting away her things Lucy sat
on the porch to wait for the paperboy.

"Hey, Lucy, you're back!" the boy shouted.

Lucy ran into the kitchen.

"Where were you?" asked Barbara. "We looked everywhere. We thought you ran away."

"We missed you so much," said Anthony.

"Looks like somebody groomed her coat," said Father.

"I think she just took a little vacation," said Mother.